For Tom and Edward *J.H.*
For Nava *E.S.*

Library of Congress Catalog Card Number 79-6703

**Library of Congress Cataloging
in Publication Data**

Hawkesworth, Jenny
The Lonely Skyscraper

Summary: A big city skyscraper, lonely when the
workers go home at night, finds a new and happy
life in the country as the home for forest animals.
[1. Skyscrapers – Fiction   2. Loneliness – Fiction]
I. Schongut, Emanuel   II. Title
PZ7.H3133LO 1980 [E] 79-6703

ISBN 0-385-15947-1 (TRADE)
ISBN 0-385-15948-X (PREBOUND)

The LONELY SKYSCRAPER

written by Jenny Hawkesworth   illustrated by Emanuel Schongut

DOUBLEDAY & COMPANY INC.,
GARDEN CITY, NEW YORK

There was once a very tall skyscraper who stood by himself in the middle of many roads. The roads went over and under each other and around and around. All the skyscraper could see was roads, stretching far into the distance.

During the day, cars and buses whizzed by and trucks thundered past in all directions.

The skyscraper was full of people who worked in him. They banged his doors and talked and laughed. They zoomed up and down in his elevators and swished in and out of his automatic doors.

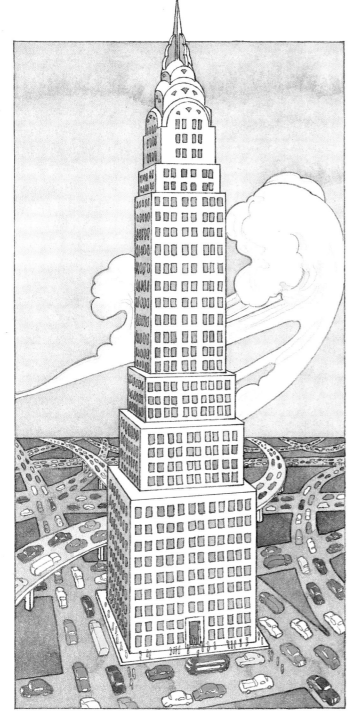

Some of the people
scrubbed and polished
him until he gleamed.
But he was always sad,
because he was nobody's
home.

At night, the skyscraper
stood alone, feeling
empty inside.
    It got cold and dark
and silent and he was
very, very lonely.

One clear day in early spring, the skyscraper was
looking at his view when, from his very top windows,
he saw something green beyond the endless gray
of the winding roads.

"I wonder what that is," he thought to himself.
He had never seen the countryside, so he didn't
know what it looked like.

But every day after that, he gazed into the
distance at the thin line of green. It looked so peaceful.

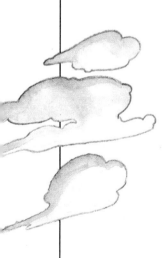

"If only I could live there," sighed the skyscraper.
One night he made up his mind to go.

First he rocked to one
side. All the pencils and
typewriters flew across
the room and crashed
against the walls.
   "OUCH!" he said.

Then he rocked to the
other side. All the
typewriters and pencils
flew back across to the
opposite walls.
   "OUCH!" he said again.

Next, he took his first step. CRUNCH! The noise of the skyscraper walking was louder than the noise of all the cars and trucks put together.

By sunrise, he had walked across all the gray roads and had just reached the beginning of the countryside that he was longing to see.

For the first time in his life, the skyscraper heard birds singing and smelled fresh, spring flowers. The muddy country path felt cool and comfortable after walking on the hard city streets.

As the sun rose, so did the skyscraper's spirits. BOOM! CRASH! TINKLE! he went, as he walked along. The sun's beams glinted and flashed on his many windows. If he'd known how to whistle he certainly would have, from sheer happiness.

Soon he came to a field with a stream running around it and some sleepy, black and white cows munching on the thick grass.

"What a lovely place to live!" thought the skyscraper, and he walked right through the fence into the middle of the field.

"Help!" cried the cows. "A monster!" and they all ran away.

An angry farmer with a red face came running down the road, waving a large stick.

"Get off my land!" he shouted, and he beat his stick against the skyscraper's gleaming front door. Of course, the skyscraper hardly noticed the stick, but he didn't like feeling unwanted, so he moved away slowly.

"Where can I go?" he wondered. "I'm too big to live here." He felt huge and ugly in the pretty green field.

Suddenly a voice said, "Don't tread on me!"
  The skyscraper bent down his top floors and
gazed at the ground. He saw a tiny brown bird.
  "I'll show you a place to live," said the bird.
"It's the most beautiful place in the world.
Let me come in and I'll take you there."

SWOOSH! The skyscraper opened his shiny door
and the little bird hopped in.

    As spring turned into summer, they traveled on.
When it rained, the skyscraper went BOOM!
SPLASH! TINKLE! SPLOSH! through all the
muddy puddles.

At last they came to a great forest.
   "Here we are!" cried the little bird.
   "How shall I get through all those trees?" asked
the skyscraper. But the trees bent aside to let him
pass and he went BOOM! TINKLE! CRUNCH!
SWISH! over the grassy floor.

They came to a space in the middle of the forest.
   "This will do," said the little bird, so the skyscraper
sat down. KERUMP! BOOM! BUMP!
   Then he arranged himself comfortably on the
moss and looked around in all directions to see what
was near him.

From his front windows,
he saw rolling hills
with sheep and cattle
grazing quietly in the
afternoon sun.

From one side, he saw
the sea, with fishing
boats and seagulls, and
a steamer trailing smoke
along the horizon.

From the other side,
he saw a village with
leafy lanes winding
among small cottages
and gardens full of
pretty flowers.

Far behind him, he saw
the gray line of the
distant city.

"So much to see and
hear and smell,"
thought the skyscraper.

When summer was over,
birds arrived to nest
in his trays.
   Squirrels stored nuts
in his paper cups.

Mice lived in drawers
and cabinets. Badgers
slept on sofas, and
moles tunnelled under
the thick carpets.

At bedtime, rabbits wrapped their babies in typewriter ribbons. Small insects were bathed in the inkwells.

Young mice cut their teeth on files marked **IMPORTANT** and the little ones were tucked into all sorts of beds.

The skyscraper soon got used to all the furry tickles and bumps, but one winter day there seemed to be more activity than usual.

"What is happening now?" he asked the little brown bird.

"We're getting ready for a party," she replied. "A skyscraper-warming party!"

"I'm warm enough already," said the skyscraper, who did not feel the cold with all the animals inside him. But the bird had already flown off to find her friends.

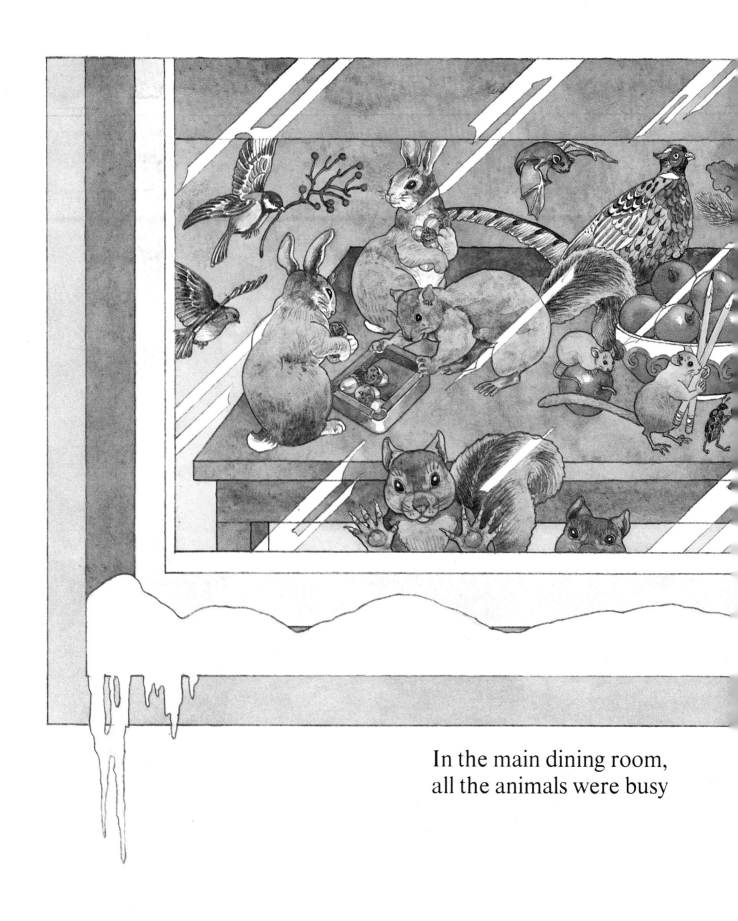

In the main dining room,
all the animals were busy

laying out a tempting feast
on the shiny table tops.

Before long, the skyscraper began to glow in the dazzling light of the setting sun. It was time for the party to begin.

Soon, sounds of merry-making rang through the snowy forest and the skyscraper was amazed to find himself growing warmer and warmer. It was a special sort of warmth, which spread from his top floors right down to his basement. Even his drafty halls felt snug, and his windy staircase, cozy.

He remembered when he had stood by himself at night feeling cold, sad and lonely.

Now he knew what a "skyscraper-warming" party really meant.

 At last he was somebody's HOME.